SERIOUSLY SILLY

SCARY
FAIRY TALES

CINDERELLA
at the
VAMPIRE BALL

Laurence Anholt
& Arthur Robins

ORCHARD

www.anholt.co.uk

GOOD EVENING, LADIES AND
GENTLEMEN.

My name is
THE MAN WITHOUT A HEAD.

It's a very silly name because if I didn't
have a head I wouldn't be talking to you now.
I have a perfectly nice head, thank you.
It's just that my head is...detachable.
It makes it easier to comb my moustache.

The stories I am about to tell are so
TERRIFYING that grown men have been
known to do wee-wees in their panties.

Perhaps you are one of those people who
believe vampire stories are for suckers?
I think my little story may change
your mind.

Are you sitting comfortably, Fans of Fear?
Tonight's tale is...

CINDERELLA AT THE VAMPIRE BALL.

There was once a girl named Ella who wasn't afraid of anything.

She loved scary stories and frightening films and her favourite day was Halloween. Her friends trembled and shivered and hid their eyes, but Ella just giggled at ghosts and sniggered at spooks.

"Nothing scares me," she said.

So when her father got remarried and took Ella to meet her new stepmother and stepsisters, Ella wasn't nervous at all.

As they drove up a long dark street named Dead End Drive, Ella whistled a happy tune.

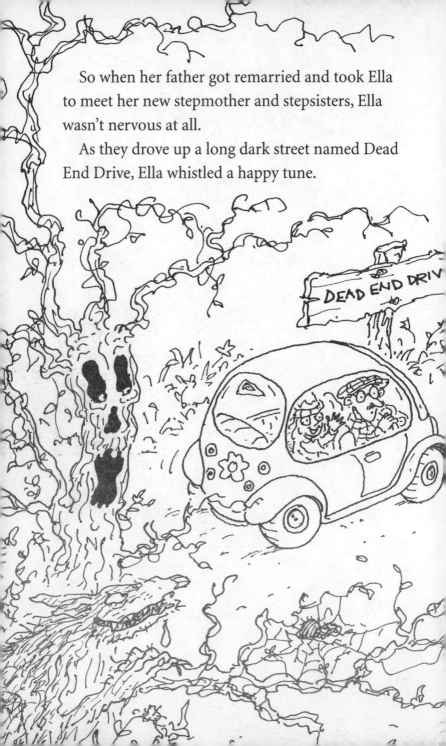

As they reached the old house with bats circling around the tall towers, Ella just unwrapped a sweetie and popped it in her mouth.

When Ella's father heaved open the huge creaking door and gently pushed Ella into the cold hallway, Ella looked around and said, "This house is weird. But I'm not scared."

"Look, Ella," said her father, "here come your new stepsisters."

Then the strangest girls that Ella had ever seen came slowly down the stairs...

"Hello, Ella," they said.

"I'm Weirdy."

"And I'm Beardy."

"Hi!" said Ella. "Let's watch TV."

The sisters shuffled into the sitting room and there, in a huge armchair, sat Ella's stepmother.

"Hello, Ella," she said. "My name is Mommy Zombie."

Ella shook her hand, but Mommy Zombie's arm
fell off.

"Don't worry, dear," said Mommy Zombie.
"We'll soon stick it back on."

"Cool," said Ella. "I'm not scared."

So Ella moved into the weird house. The
bedrooms were damp and cold, so Ella curled
up with the bats and the cats and the rats in the
cinders by the fire. Then everyone called her
Cinderella.

Weirdy and Beardy had lots of horrible habits – they kept leaving arms and legs and other bits of their bodies lying around the house. Once Ella found someone's head sitting in the sink.

"Boo!" said the head.

"I'm not scared," said Cinderella.

Cinderella's stepsisters gave her all the frightening jobs to do. But Cinderella didn't mind.

Not even when she had to clean the cobwebs in the dark, dark cellar...

Hey! Get out of my website!

Mine's a bloodhound!

Not even when she had to walk the zombie dogs in the zombie park...

I want my deady bear

Quick! Turn on the dark, Cinderella we're afraid of the light!

Not even when she had to tuck her stepsisters into bed in their tall, tall tower...

One day a pale postman knocked on the door. With trembling fingers he handed Weirdy a black envelope. Then he ran down the drive as fast as his legs would carry him.

"Ooh, look!" said Beardy. "It's an invitation from Count Jugular."

"Who's Count Jugular?" said Cinderella.

"Don't you know?" said Weirdy. "Count Jugular is the vampire prince. He's the most handsome man alive. Or should I say, the most handsome man...dead! We are both members of his fang club."

Then the sisters laughed their heads off.

Cinderella read the invitation.

COUNT JUGULAR INVITES YOU TO A
VAMPIRE BALL

WHERE? JUGULAR CASTLE.

WHEN? FANGSGIVING DAY.

TIME? THE MIDDLE OF THE FRIGHT.

WHY? HE'S LOOKING FOR A
GHOULFRIEND TO BE HIS BRIDE.

WHO? SHE MIGHT BE A PRINCESS OR
JUST THE GIRL NECKS DOOR.

PLEASE TICK:

YES I CAN COME. I'M DEAD EXCITED ☐

NO I CAN'T COME. I'M GRAVELY ILL ☐

Weirdy and Beardy were terribly excited about the vampire ball. They were both sure that Count Jugular would choose them to be his ghoulfriend.

Now, as I have told you, Cinderella wasn't scared of anything. But for some reason, she seemed a little nervous. "I think I'd rather stay at home and watch a scary movie," she said.

"Surely, you're not scared of a vampire ball?" asked Mommy Zombie.

"Of course not," said Cinderella. "Vampires are just a pain in the neck!"

Weirdy, Beardy and Mommy Zombie spent ages getting ready.

Cinderella's dad said he would drive the girls to Castle Jugular; so Cinderella stayed alone with the cats and the bats and the rats by the fire.

The house seemed dark and quiet without her stepsisters. Then Cinderella heard a low moaning, like the wind in the chimney. "Whoo-whoo!"

"Whoever you are, I'm not scared," said Cinderella.

"Whoo-whoo!" said the voice again.

Suddenly Cinderella saw a ghostly white figure beside her.

"Boo!" said the spook.

"Boo to you too," said Cinderella. "I'm not scared."

"I am your Fairy Ghostmother," said the ghost. "I've just come home from work and I'm dead on my feet."

"You do look a little pale," said Cinderella. "Where do ghosts work, anyway?"

"In the morning I work with the tiny ghosties at the Day Scare Centre and in the afternoon I work at the Ghost Office. Now, why are you sitting on your own?"

"Everyone has gone to the Vampire Ball," said Cinderella. "And I wish I had gone after all. It's dead boring here."

"Well guess what, Cinders? You shall go to the ball. You'll have a wail of a time."

"But what shall I wear, Fairy Ghostmother? I need something really vampy."

"It's time for a spooky spell," said the Fairy Ghostmother. She began to wail and moan and wave her arms about.

*"Dress this girl from head to toes
In SERIOUSLY SCARY party clothes!"*

Cinderella looked in the mirror. She couldn't believe her eyes. She was dressed in a beautiful velvet ballgown with red trimmings.

"Oh, Fairy Ghostmother, I feel booo-tiful!"

"That's the spirit. And look, here's a pair of glass booo-ties for your little feet."

"Oh, but Fairy Ghostmother, how will I get to the ball?" asked Cinderella.

"Just bring me six black bats," said her Fairy Ghostmother. "It's time for another spooky spell."

"Listen, Cinders, here's the deal
You'll go to the ball in a BATMOBILE!"

Outside the door stood a gleaming black coach pulled by six vampire bats.

"Oh, thank you, Fairy Ghostmother," she said.

But her Fairy Ghostmother had one important warning.

*"Leave by midnight, please be wary
Or things may turn out
SERIOUSLY SCARY!"*

"Yeah, whatever." said Cinderella. "I'm not scared."
Then she hopped into the black coach and set off
flying and swooping through the moonlit sky, high
above the city, until she could see the dark towers of
Castle Jugular far below.

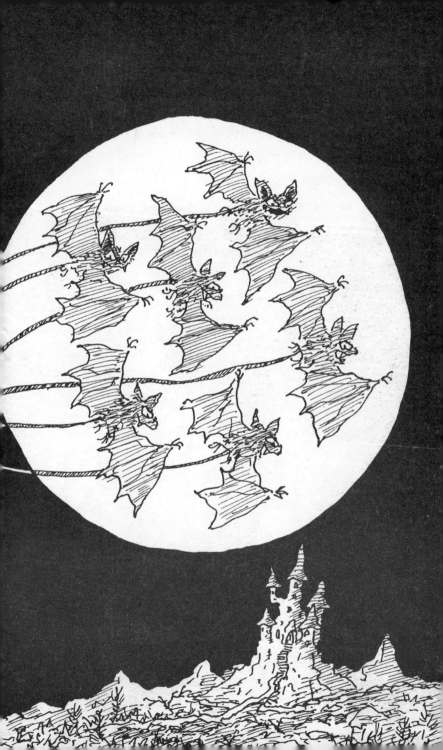

Cinderella parked the Batmobile in the car park. Then she climbed the steps to the castle doors. In a huge ballroom, a hundred strange people were dancing to a skeleton band.

Cinderella spotted her father waltzing with Mommy Zombie. And there were Weirdy and Beardy throwing their bodies around the dance floor. Cinderella was just about to join them when she noticed a very handsome young man by the food table.

The man had glossy black hair and lovely shiny teeth. As soon as he saw Cinderella, his red eyes shone.

"I am Count Jugular," he said, taking her arm. "Come and have a bite to eat. Would you like a stake sandwich? Or a Fangfurter? There's plenty to get your teeth into."

"No thanks. I'm a vegetarian," said Cinderella.

"Well, how about some fruit?" he said. "Have a necktarine."

"You know what?" said Cinderella. "I don't feel very hungry."

"Well, then let's dance," said Count Jugular.
"Listen. They're playing my favourite song –
'You're So Vein'."

So Cinderella danced with the Count and the
hours slipped away.

"You have such a beautiful long neck," said Count Jugular. "And now it's almost midnight...it's time to choose my bride..."

"Eeek!" squealed Cinderella. "There's only one thing that scares me...I really, really, really DON'T WANNA GET MARRIED!"

Then she ran out of the ballroom and away
down the steps.

"Wait for us!" called Weirdy and Beardy. "That
party was dead boring, anyway."

As the clock struck midnight, the three sisters held hands and ran into the night.

Weirdy ran so fast that her foot fell off. "Don't worry," she said, "I'll fetch it in the morning."

"Phew!" said Cinderella as they arrived home.
"That was the scariest thing I ever heard."

Next morning, there was a loud knock at the door. Cinderella went to answer it and there stood Count Jugular.

"I hate coming out in the light," he said, "but whoever fits this foot will be my ghoulfriend."

"Well, I'm wearing both my feet," said Cinderella. "It must be one of my stepsisters."

"It's me, it's me!" shouted Weirdy. "I'm going to be Jugular's bride."

"And we'll be bridesmaids!" said Mommy
Zombie, Beardy and the Fairy Ghostmother.

"And I'll go too of course," said Cinderella. "It will be the ghastliest, ghostliest, creepiest, spookiest, weirdest wedding of all time. But I'm not scared."

SERIOUSLY SILLY

SCARY
FAIRY TALES

LAURENCE ANHOLT & ARTHUR ROBINS

Cinderella at the Vampire Ball	PB 978 1 40832 954 2
Jack and the Giant Spiderweb	PB 978 1 40832 957 3
Hansel and Gretel and the Space Witch	PB 978 1 40832 960 3
Snow Fright and the Seven Skeletons	PB 978 1 40832 963 4
Ghostyshocks and the Three Mummies	PB 978 1 40832 966 5
Tom Thumb, the Tiny Spook	PB 978 1 40832 969 6

COLLECT THEM ALL!

Also available
as an ebook